Johnny Germ Head

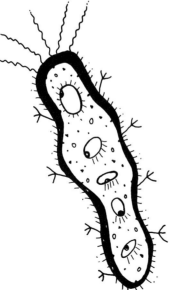

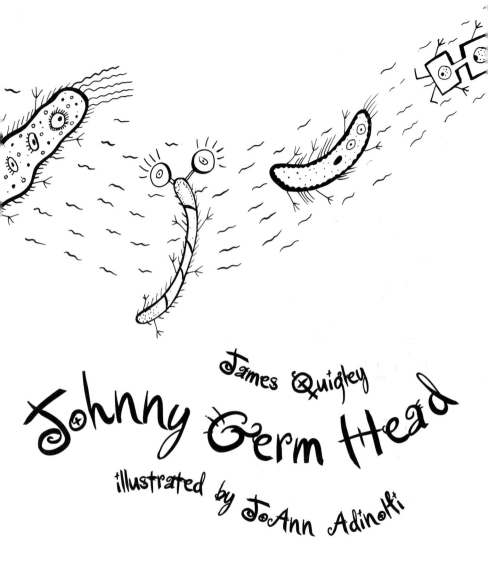

James Quigley

Johnny Germ Head

illustrated by JoAnn Adinolfi

A Redfeather Book

Henry Holt and Company New York

Henry Holt and Company, Inc.
Publishers since 1866
115 West 18th Street
New York, New York 10011

Henry Holt is a registered
trademark of Henry Holt and Company, Inc.

Published in Canada by Fitzhenry & Whiteside Ltd.,
195 Allstate Parkway, Markham, Ontario L3R 4T8.

Library of Congress Cataloging-in-Publication Data
Quigley, James.
 Johnny Germ Head / by James Quigley; illustrated by JoAnn Adinolfi.
  p.   cm.—(A Redfeather Book)
 Summary: While performing a heroic act at an amusement park, third-
grader Johnny Jarvis finally confronts the fear of germs that had been an
obsession with him ever since he was seven.
 [1. Hypochondria—Fiction. 2. Microorganisms—Fiction. 3. Fear—
Fiction.] I. Adinolfi, JoAnn, ill. II. Title. III. Series: Redfeather Books.
PZ7.Q4154Jo 1997 [E]—dc21   97–11294

ISBN 0-8050-5395-6
First Edition—1997
Designed by Meredith Baldwin
Digital font copyright ©1997 by Dave McKean
Printed in Mexico

10 9 8 7 6 5 4 3 2 1

For Mom
—J. Q.

To my cousins Steven, Amanda, and Nicole
—J. A.

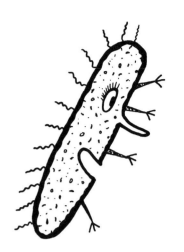

Contents

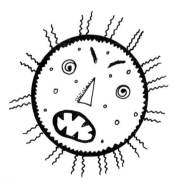

Johnny Germ Head

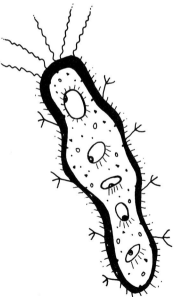

Killer T's on the Prowl

My real name is Johnny Jarvis, but the kids at school call me Johnny Germ Head.

I first started worrying about germs last year when I was seven. It happened after I told my mom and dad I wanted to be a doctor. The next thing you know, they gave me a microscope and a couple of books on biology and the human body. Mom even took me to the laboratory where she works peering through her big microscope. All of a sudden her constant warnings about germs took on a new meaning.

They were everywhere, squirming and wriggling. You could look at a glob of mayonnaise spilled on the kitchen counter and see nothing but white goo. But put that glob under a microscope and there, before your very eyes, was a gang of happy germs just chomping away like people in a cafeteria. The scary thing was that these germs were *living creatures*. Sure, their bodies were tiny, but they were alive just the same. And boy could these critters make you sick.

The more I read my books, the more frightened I became. It was terrifying to think that I had billions of germs living inside of me. But at least I had my immune system to protect me.

The way I see it, the immune system is like an army of soldiers in your body that chases away germs. Sometimes the soldiers arrest the germs after they get inside, then they put the germs in prison or kick them out of your body. And once the immune system soldiers see a bad germ, they remember that germ's face forever. If the germ is crazy enough to try to get back into your body, the soldiers attack it on the spot.

I decided that I needed more information about the immune system if I was going to beat these germs, so I went to the library and took out a huge book called *Soldiers of the Immune System*. Soon I started to understand

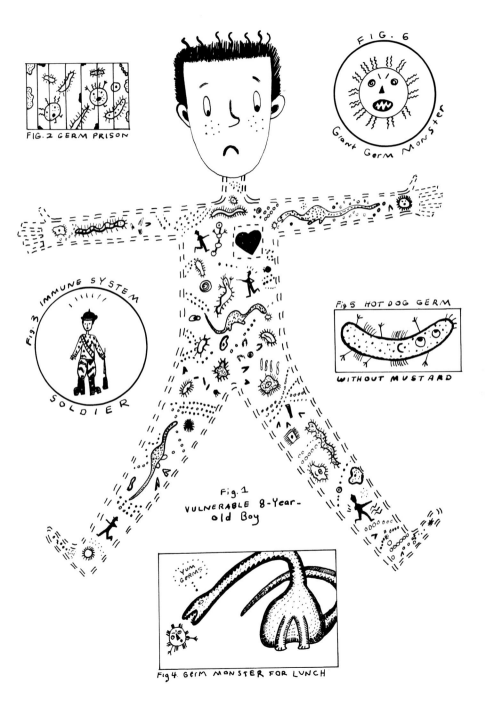

FIG. 2 GERM PRISON

FIG. 6 Giant Germ Monster

Fig. 3 IMMUNE SYSTEM SOLDIER

Fig 5 HOT DOG GERM
WITHOUT MUSTARD

Fig. 1
VULNERABLE 8-Year-old Boy

YUM GERMS

Fig 4 GERM MONSTER FOR LUNCH

a little about "Killer T cells," the special cells that fight germs.

The name *Killer T cell* reminded me of *Tyrannosaurus rex*. That's because scientists sometimes call Tyrannosaurus rex "T. rex." He was a killer dinosaur. I began thinking of the entire immune system as this army of dinosaurs, and my insides as the land where the dinosaurs lived. Say some kid at school sneezed and wiped his hand all over the basketball—these globular, tentacled germ-monsters with crazy eyes and mouthfuls of teeth would launch an attack. The dinosaurs, led by Tyrannosaurus rexes, would charge out to meet them, fangs bared. There would be a battle, with germ-monsters and dinosaurs tearing and clawing each other. The dinosaurs would always win.

What scares me the most is that one of these days the dinosaurs might not win.

Panic Attack

It's already the end of May and the school year is almost over. Since there's not a lot of schoolwork left for us to do, Mrs. Guildersleeve tells us to bring in some books to read. I bring in *A Field Guide to Symptoms*, by Dr. Eeyore Sickmann. At lunch, I show my book to my friend David and some of the other guys. They stop talking about David's book on sharks and look at mine.

"A symptom is something you get that might mean you have a disease," I explain. "This book lists all the symptoms there are and it tells you what diseases go with them."

Some of the guys find this hard to believe.

"It's true," I insist. "Suppose you feel dizzy—that could mean you're sick. Have you ever felt dizzy?"

Everybody—and I mean the whole entire class—runs down the hall, away from where David was standing. Some kids even go straight down the stairs and out the school door. The rest of us wait at the end of the hall for Mrs. Guildersleeve to return. It seems as if the spot where he got sick is radioactive and nobody wants to go anywhere near it.

Caitlin Hernandez comes up to me. "You're in trouble, Johnny Germ Head."

Caitlin is always giving me grief. "Why?" I ask.

"For making us run all the way down the hall."

"I didn't make you run. Go back if you want. I'm sure the germs will be happy to see you. They're looking for a place to live."

Caitlin shakes her head, but she doesn't go back.

"Johnny, what's wrong with David?" Naomi Dale asks.

"I think it has something to do with his brain," I say. "Or maybe it's the flu. I sure hope he's okay."

Mr. Kyle, who teaches fourth grade, comes out of his classroom and sees us in the hall. He tries to take us back to our classroom, but we won't go until the janitor cleans up the mess.

"And tell him to use bleach, Mr. Kyle," I say. "That's the best way to kill the germs. Soap just makes it smell nice. And have him spray Germ-Be-Gone disinfectant in the air to knock out the microbes that are already airborne."

Mr. Kyle sighs and goes off to find the janitor.

When everything is cleaned up, we file back into the classroom. Mrs. Guildersleeve returns and tells us that David is going home.

At the end of the day, when all the kids are busy drawing pictures for art class, Mrs. Guildersleeve calls me up to her desk. I figure she's going to congratulate me for leading all the other kids out of danger, but I'm wrong.

"Johnny, do you think that maybe you caused a panic today when you told your classmates that they might catch germs from David?"

"No, Mrs. Guildersleeve. A panic is when people don't have a good reason to get excited. But those germs! My gosh, I could practically smell them! We all had to get away, quick. That's why I told everybody to run. The germs were preparing to attack. I could hear them buzzing in the air. Did you want us all to get sick like David? Germs spread fast. The whole school would have gotten sick in an hour. We would have needed a hundred janitors working for a whole week with a thousand gallons of bleach—"

Mrs. Guildersleeve put her hand up and I know that means I have to stop talking and listen.

"Johnny, you're going to *make* yourself sick by thinking about germs all the time. That's what happened to David. He made himself sick after reading your book."

"But maybe he really has some crazy disease! The flu is going around, you know."

"He doesn't have a disease, it was all in his head. Oh, Johnny, why don't you stop thinking about germs? At least for the summer."

"I'll try. I promise."

Mrs. Guildersleeve smiles and gives me a wink.

The funny thing is I really mean it.

Blocking Out the Sun

But I soon learn that it's one thing to *want* to stop thinking about germs, and another thing to actually *stop* thinking about them. There are reminders every-where: doorknobs, forks with dishwasher spots on them, people's hands, relatives slobbering you with kisses, and of course the bathroom, a germ's favorite place. And then there's *A Field Guide to Symptoms*. Try as I might, I can't stop reading it. Before I know it, I've been on summer vacation a whole week and all I've done is read my book—cover to cover. Summer has hardly begun and I've already given up. The germs have won, and Kraft Kamp is just around the corner. I wish I could get out of going, but Mom signed me up months ago.

I hear Mom coming up the stairs and I quickly hide

"Aw, Mom—" She literally grabs me by the arm, drags me downstairs, and throws me out of the house. I can't believe it. She's never done this before. I ring the doorbell ten times, but she doesn't answer. Dad can't hear the bell because he's in the basement grunting away on his exercise machine. I run around to the back door and pound on it with my fist. I see Sammy inside.

"Hey, Sammy, open the door! Let me in!"

Sammy smiles, and runs away. I dash around to the window of Mom's study, which is on the ground level. She's in there, hunched behind her computer. Maybe if I had been on my computer she wouldn't have kicked me out. She obviously thinks lying around is a waste of time on a sunny day like today.

"Mom!" I call. "I need sunblock and my hat!"

I see her get up, a ghostly shadow moving in the window's sun-glare. After a few minutes an upstairs window opens and Mom throws out a bottle of sunblock and my hat that says "Germ Free" on it (I ordered it from the Germ-Be-Gone Disinfectant Company).

I smear the sunblock on extra thick all over my face,

can all go swimming in clean water with lots of chlorine that kills the germs." She makes a shot from back near her parents' car. Then she passes the ball to me. I shoot from where Naomi was standing, but the basketball sails clear over the backboard and rolls across the lawn.

"Air ball!" Caitlin shouts. She scoops up the stray basketball, dribbles it, and makes a nice layup.

"There are more germs in a pool," I say, "than in a lake. Pools use the same water over and over and maintenance changes it probably once the whole summer. The chlorine only kills the wimpy germs."

Naomi and Caitlin give me a dirty look. "That's not true," Naomi snaps.

"Yes it is," I reply sadly. "And in two days we're all going to be taking a swim with those same supergerms. Get ready to get sick."

Germ Soup and Slime Stew

Of course, the first thing they make you do at Kraft Kamp is take a swim test in the new pool.

"I don't want to swim," I tell Tom, one of the counselors.

"Everyone has to take the test," Tom says. "No exceptions. You'll be fine."

"But all I want to do is make things out of wood and clay. I'm not going to drown in the Kraft Lodge."

"Camp rules," says Tom. "Everybody has to take the swim test. It's the law around here."

"You used to want to be a lifeguard," says David, who's standing next to me getting ready to take the test. "Why are you suddenly afraid of the water?"

"I'm not afraid of the water. I'm afraid of what's *in* the water."

"What's in the water?" David chuckles. "Sharks?"

I roll my eyes. "Not sharks. Germs!"

"You and your germs! You're acting crazy," blurts David, and he turns away. But I know I've got him thinking.

The row of kids in front of us finishes the test. They leave the pool, dripping wet and breathing hard. A counselor pats them on the back. I'm up next. Somehow I've got to get through this.

Tom gives the command. Everyone else jumps in, but my feet stay planted in the ground.

"What are you waiting for?" Tom asks.

"Are you sure there's enough chlorine in this pool?" I ask, hoping to buy some time. "Why don't we use the lake anymore?"

Caitlin is chattering away with Naomi, who is next in line, but suddenly stops talking. "Move it, Johnny!" Caitlin yells, as she gives me a swift push from behind.

SPLASH!

I'm a goner. The invisible enemies are all around me. I've got to get through this as soon as possible. When Tom tells us to swim freestyle across the pool, I take a deep breath and try to keep my mouth shut. As I'm swimming, my lungs feel like they're about to burst. At the end of my lap, David splashes me in the face just as I gasp for air, and I swallow a mouthful of water.

It occurs to me that the pool isn't just filled with germs that live there year-round, but also with new germs brought in by the campers, like chicken pox and ringworm or even strep throat. I bet there's a huge germ convention in the swimming pool, and germs hug and kiss old germ friends and discuss new ways to make people sick.

As I take the other tests, like the dead man's float, I keep telling myself, *It's almost over, it's almost over.* The whole time I can sense the germs sizing me up, like killer whales circling around a wounded blue whale. But what can I do? I have no choice. Like Tom says, the swim test is the law.

It's a good thing I act calm in the pool, because I end

up passing. It must have been all that mind control and deep breathing. I get a Gold Fish rating, which means I can go swimming whenever I want. Of course, I never will go swimming if I can help it. David gets a Silver Fish rating, which means he has to take daily swimming lessons. What a drag.

"Lucky duck," he says.

"I'd give you my Gold Fish rating if I could," I answer. "It's the last thing I'll use."

That night I go to bed hoping that maybe there are fewer germs up in the mountains than there are in the suburbs. Maybe even the pool is safe.

But the following morning, I wake up with a sore throat. To me that means only one thing: the pool *was* teeming with germs after all. Yesterday I took a dip in a huge pot of germ soup.

The nurse tells me that it's probably just allergies, but I bet it's strep throat. I'm not going anywhere near that pool. And if I have to walk by it, I'll hold my breath.

*   *   *

For the next few days, I spend all my time in the Kraft lodges, especially the Pottery Lodge, where I'm making a battlefield of dinosaurs and germs out of clay. All the dinosaurs look like T. rexes, and the germs look like octopuses, squid, and crabs. A few look like werewolves and centipedes. All of them have more than two eyes. I also make big fuzz-balls with lots of teeth for pollen, and leaves with six legs for poison ivy. I even make a purple manta ray with a poisonous stinger for an ultraviolet ray. Then I give them names like Thoggle, Splicker, Vragon, and Superdooper-sickermaker.

The flu is their leader. As a joke, I make it look like David. But David gets mad, so I change it to a big praying mantis.

Soon, more and more camp counselors come by to admire my battlefield. When I tell them it's called "Germs Versus the Immune System," they give me a funny look, but they still like it. The counselors move the whole thing to the center of the lodge, and all the kids stop by to see it.

of a bat and put it on the battlefield. Every possible germ and bad thing I can think of is on that battlefield fighting my dinosaurs.

Afterward, I decide to go find Naomi and Caitlin in the woods. I make sure to walk at an easy pace so I don't get heatstroke. It's actually pretty nice in the woods, if you just keep an eye out for poison ivy and ticks.

I hear some racket nearby, and sure enough, there are Caitlin and Naomi preparing to put up their homes for dangerous flying animals.

"There's Johnny!" yells Caitlin. "He came to help us put up the bat boxes."

"Come on over," Naomi calls.

But I don't walk over. The trail goes straight through a big patch of poison ivy.

"Is there some other way of getting over there without having to go through these bad boys?" I point to the poison ivy.

"What bad boys?" asks Caitlin.

"This poison ivy."

"That's not poison ivy," she says.

"Are you sure?"

"Of course. I'm a Girl Scout, I know my poison ivy."

"I don't know, that looks like poison ivy to me."

"Naomi!" calls Caitlin. "Is that poison ivy?"

Naomi comes up, takes one quick look at the patch, and shouts, "No. Definitely not poison ivy!"

Just the same, I know to take precautions. First I roll down my jeans' cuffs and tuck them into my socks. Then I pull the socks up as far as they will go. It's goofy looking, but at least I'm protected.

As I tiptoe through the patch, the poison ivy leaves resemble evil faces of goblins eager to bite into my legs and inject their poison. I shudder. *Just make it to the other side*, I keep telling myself.

"Are you sure that's not poison ivy?" I ask Caitlin when I reach her. "Maybe you should double-check."

Caitlin looks at the leaves again. "No," she repeats. "It's not poison ivy. Oh my gosh! I think it's poison sumac!"

"Aw, Caitlin! How could you make that mistake?"

"Don't worry, Johnny. Poison sumac is not nearly as strong as poison ivy, right, Naomi?"

"I thought it was the other way around," Naomi mumbles.

There's no time to waste. Without saying good-bye I rush back to my bunk and undress. I try to do this without touching the part of my clothes that might have touched the poison sumac. Normally I wear flip-flops in the shower, but I can't find them in the heat of the moment. I jump into the shower and scrub so hard I nearly rub off my outer layer of skin. That's fine with me, as long as the poison sumac oil gets washed away with it. Just as I'm about to dry off, my foot touches something slimy. I look down.

Mold.

The next thing I know, I'm back in the shower, scouring my foot like it's a dirty pot. But while I'm in there, I hear my towel drop off the peg and fall onto the floor. I spring out of the shower and pick it up, but I know it's too late. Athlete's foot and mold don't need much time to infect a towel. I have no choice. Wincing in horror, I wrap myself in the contaminated towel and hurry into the main part of the bunkhouse to get a clean one. Then I leap back into the shower.

I'm in there scrubbing for ten minutes. When I come out the towel is on the floor again. I bet the germs, the athlete's foot, and the poison sumac oils squirmed up the wall and pushed my towel onto the floor. Without wasting a minute more, I grab a new towel, wrap it around the peg, and rush into the shower. I don't care if I have to take a million showers. I'll fight these germs until the end.

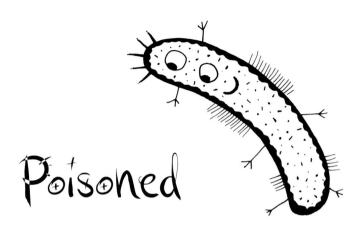

Poisoned

Despite all that trouble, I get a poison sumac rash two days after I returned home from Kraft Kamp. Maybe there was a hole in my sock. I guess walking through a patch of poison sumac and not getting a rash is like swimming across the Amazon and not being chewed to a skeleton by starving piranhas.

The rash itches terribly so I stay in bed with my leg raised and slathered with lotion.

I reach down and grab *A Field Guide to Symptoms* off the floor, even though I promised myself I would never look at that book again. There's a disease I want to check out. I've got this nagging fear that my rash isn't poison sumac but leprosy, a really awful disease that can make your nose pop off. Just then Mom comes into the room.

trees, flowers, even the president of the United States. And everywhere you go, you see noses popping off.

"Johnny, Naomi and Caitlin are here to see you!" Mom calls up the stairs.

When they come up I groan a little and lower my eyelids.

"How are you, Johnny?" Naomi asks.

"I'm feeling a little better," I answer groggily. "The poison sumac got me." I point to the lotion on my right leg.

"That little spot?" asks Caitlin.

I nod.

"That's nothing, Johnny," says Naomi. "It's only about the size of a quarter."

"We have it, too." Caitlin giggles. "But we have it all over both legs."

"It itches like you won't believe," I moan. "It itches right down to the bone."

"That's why you put lotion on it, silly," Naomi teases as she shows off the pink blotches on her legs.

"Listen, Johnny, in two weeks my brother is taking us to Kaptin Phun's Krazy Cingdum by the C. They've got three new roller coasters: the Tipsy Sailor, the Sea Serpent, and the Giant Squid. Want to go? My brother's got a bunch of free tickets. David's coming, too," Naomi says.

"Sure," I answer, trying to sound excited. "If this poison sumac ever gets better."

Caitlin gives Naomi an I-told-you-so look. For some reason I'm embarrassed.

"It should be better in two weeks," Naomi remarks.

"I'll have to ask my mom," I reply.

"We already asked her. She said you could go," Naomi shoots back.

"Great!" I say enthusiastically.

But it isn't great. After they leave, I sit in bed trying to think of a way to get out of this mess. The fact is, I hate amusement parks. I never get amused by them, just sick. Not only are amusement parks swarming with germs, but the germs have more fun than the people. They hop around in the food, hide out in the rest rooms, and stick like glue to the bars of all the rides, just waiting to attack visitors. Whoever invented amusement parks must have been a germ lover.

A Glide on the Wild Ride

Those two weeks flash by like lightning. The day before our trip to Kaptin Phun's, I wrack my brain but I can't think of an excuse not to go.

That night in bed, I can hardly sleep a wink. I have a nightmare about a roller coaster flying off the track and crashing into a gigantic heap of infected hospital waste. Waking up in a cold sweat, I switch on the radio to calm my nerves. But there's a show on about Ebola, this horrible virus that kills you in a couple of days. I know I shouldn't listen, that I should change the station right away, but I can't. That's the problem with thinking about germs all the time—even though you're petrified that you're going to catch different diseases, you can't help but listen when you hear someone talking about the symptoms.

Ebola is the worst. A voice on the radio describes an Ebola victim's symptoms, which sound like something from a science fiction movie. I imagine that when you catch Ebola, you turn into a big blob of goo that explodes all over the place. Entire villages become blobified. The people run out in terror and blobify the guards who are trying to keep them in the villages. It happened to this guy on a plane. There he was, eating his peanuts and reading his airline magazine, and all of a sudden he became blobified. And the worst thing of all is this: it spreads like wildfire in places where there are a lot of people in close contact. *Places like amusement parks!* I think to myself.

I force myself to turn off the radio before the announcer finishes telling the story. Maybe it was just a late-night radio show where they make up creepy stories for their listeners. But maybe not. I'm so scared I can't even close my eyes. Ebola is the big one. It's like the giant asteroid that wiped out the dinosaurs.

When morning comes, I'm still lying there, wide awake with my eyes bugged out like a goldfish. I put on my sunblock, my Germ Free cap, and slip my portable first-aid kit into my pocket. Mom makes me breakfast and tries to get me excited about Kaptin Phun's Krazy Cingdum because she knows I don't really want to go. Sammy is pouting because he has to stay behind.

"Believe me," I say to him, "you're the lucky one."

Naomi's brother, Noah, picks me up at nine o'clock. Noah is sitting up front with his girlfriend. I sit in the back with David, Caitlin, and Naomi. David looks at me, then turns away and shakes his head.

"Why are you wearing that dumb cap?" gripes David.

"It keeps the sun off my head." It also keeps stray germs from entering my ears, but if I tell David that, he'll think I'm *completely* nuts.

David doesn't say anything, but I can tell he's worried about going around with a guy who's wearing a Germ Free cap. Too bad.

"Ready for the Sea Serpent, Johnny?" asks Caitlin.

"Sure," I lie.

"I don't know if we'll go on that first," she continues. "Maybe we'll try out the Tipsy Sailor or the Giant Squid. Laura Hart said the Sea Serpent was better than the Giant Squid, but Maria Recca said the Giant Squid is the best. She saw a kid throw up on it." Caitlin looks at me and smiles.

"Cool," I mutter. "A kid threw up."

Naomi and Caitlin pull out their roller coaster log-books and compare notes. It turns out that they've been keeping track of all the roller coasters they've ever been on. Next to each roller coaster, they put how many times they've been on it and whether it was Bad, Medium, Good, or Excellent. It's probably the sickest hobby I've ever heard of, and I know *sick*.

"The Hurler at Duke's Dominion was the best so far," announces Naomi, consulting her notes.

"I liked the Dragon Coaster at Playland," remarks Caitlin. "I went on it five times."

"Adventure Zone had some good ones, too," adds Naomi. "Have you been to Adventure Zone, Johnny?"

"Yeah. I like the safari."

"Did you get out of the car and show the animals your hat?" taunts David.

"I sure did," I reply. "In fact one of the animals looked just like you. In the hyena section."

David shakes his head, as if my comeback was stupid, but Caitlin laughs.

It takes almost two hours to get to the amusement park. Once we get through the gates with our free tickets, Noah tells us to stick together. "If anybody gets lost, you should meet here by Kaptin Phun's Giant Treasure Chest. We'll meet here again at one o'clock. See you guys later."

"Great," I grumble to Naomi. "Your brother's not staying with us?"

"I guess not," she says. "But that's better."

"Suppose it rains and we catch pneumonia, how will Noah know to take us home?" I ask.

"Johnny, relax. Try to forget about germs for a while. This is going to be a great day. Let's find the Sea Serpent," Naomi responds.

Of course we can't start off with some easy ride, like

the log flume. We've got to hit the Sea Serpent first. I moan to myself. According to our map, the Sea Serpent is somewhere at the other end of the park.

We follow the map along the winding paths of the park. The ground is sticky from all the spilled ice cream and soda. A shiver runs down my spine as I think of the germs clinging to the soles of my shoes. I'll have to remember to blast them with Germ-Be-Gone spray when I get home.

If there's one thing I hate almost as much as the dirty rides and germs at an amusement park, it's grown men and women wandering around in costumes harassing kids. Kaptin Phun is no exception. He seems to spot us fifty yards away. The next thing you know, he's standing right next to us in his red pirate coat and his black hat, waving a floppy rubber sword. A person in a giant parrot costume is bobbing up and down next to him.

"Arrrrr, shipmates," he says in this growling voice. "Welcome to me Krazy Cingdum by the C! Be that a treasure map ye got there?" Spit flies out of the Kaptin's mouth as he talks.

I quickly jump backward.

"Lend an ear, matey," the Kaptin shouts. "A li'l spit never hurt anybody. Ye can't be a seafarin' man if ye don't like the spit of the frothy waves against yer cheeks!"

"Blech," I gag.

Naomi and Caitlin look at each other and giggle. People stand around and smile. Little kids point at Kaptin Phun and the giant parrot. David's face turns red. For once I feel the same way he does. This is humiliating. And dangerous. Not only is the Kaptin a spitting menace, but those costumes are sure to be infested with germs from all their contact with the crowds of people. And the inside of that plastic parrot mask must be a steam bath where germs breed by the billions.

"Pieces of eight! Pieces of eight!" screeches the giant parrot. Someone in an ape costume comes up and pounds his chest. "Bugga, bugga, bugga!"

Another walking germ factory. They're everywhere!

Naomi and Caitlin, and a lot of the people standing around, think this is hysterical. I try to make my escape but Kaptin Phun catches me.

"And where ye be slinkin', shipmate?"

"Get away from me," I mutter.

"Arrrrr, matey, them's fightin' words. I'll see you on the poop!"

As we move on, the gigantic Sea Serpent gradually comes into view. The roller coaster is on an island surrounded by a moat of the most grimy water I've ever seen. It has two giant drops, three loops, and a spiral, and at one point you actually come close to getting sprayed with the putrid moat water!

A pit forms in my stomach when I think about the safety bar you have to grasp when you're on the ride. It's worse than a doorknob because it gets touched by hundreds of people every day. Hour after hour people stream on and off the rides, wiping the safety bar with their unwashed hands, sneezing on it, and maybe even spitting on it like Kaptin Phun.

The germs probably line up for hands just like people line up to get on the roller coaster. I shake my head and tell myself I'll be all right.

When it's our turn to get on the ride, I sit next to Naomi, close my eyes, put my hat between my knees, and brace my feet against the front of the car. Then I suck in my breath and grab the bar. I can feel the germs burrowing into my skin as the roller coaster cranks slowly up the first hill.

I keep my eyelids shut so tight that I see flashing stars. Then it's over. No sooner am I off the ride, then I'm in the bathroom washing my hands furiously.

Revenge of the Sea Serpent

"Johnny, are you okay?" Naomi asks, concern showing on her face. I realize that she thinks I ran into the bathroom to be sick.

"I'm okay—I just had to wash the germs off." Naomi looks bothered, as if her concern had been wasted.

"You shouldn't yell so much, Johnny," huffs Caitlin.

"Why? Lots of other people yelled."

"I know, but you're supposed to stop yelling when the roller coaster comes back into the station. People will think you're weird."

"They already think he's weird. You should have seen him in the bathroom waving his hands like they were on fire," David snips.

Next we go on the Giant Squid, but this time I'm prepared. I hold on to the safety bar with paper towels from the bathroom. I do the same on the Tipsy Sailor, the Buccaneer, and all of the other rides. All the while I feel protected, because I change my paper towels between rides like a doctor changing rubber gloves between patients.

At one o'clock we meet Noah and his girlfriend and go to the Pirate's Cove Pavilion for lunch. The place gives me the creeps. I have this idea that the cooks are wild high school kids who never wash their hands and who sneeze on the food just for fun. On the other hand, I'm hungry, so I order a Pirateburger with cheese, spicy fries, and a soda. It tastes good, but that doesn't mean no germs are hitchhiking.

After lunch I grab some napkins and a packet of salt. Then I head back to the bathroom and gargle with salt water to kill any lingering germs from lunch.

On our way to the log flume, I notice a singing clown selling ice cream from a stand. His sign says Kreamy the Klown.

Now that summer's hot and steamy,
You need something cold and creamy.
Frosty shakes and sundaes yummy,
Will help to cool your hungry tummy!

"I could really go for ice cream right now," I say to everyone.

"I could, too," agrees Naomi. "Let's hurry before a long line forms."

We make a mad dash to the ice cream stand. I'm the first to order. "What would you like, young fellow?" Kreamy asks. Then he sneezes, ACHOO! and wipes his nose on his sleeve.

"Well?" he sniffles. "Kreamy has lots of frosty, scrumptious treats for you kids today!"

I wince and step back.

"Hurry up and order, Johnny," says Caitlin from behind me. "A lot of people are waiting."

"I-I'll have a Strawberrie Softie," I stammer.

"Coming right up!" Kreamy turns around and starts filling my cone with strawberry custard. He hums as he goes about his work. At least he uses a napkin to hold the cone. Suddenly he gets a funny look on his face. His eyes glaze over and his mouth opens. It looks like he's about to shout. He turns his face slightly away from my ice cream, but instead of shouting, he starts coughing. It sounds like a wild animal is barking in his chest. Not only that, but his germs are spraying all over my ice-cream cone. When his coughing fit is over, Kreamy hands me my cone. I take it with my left hand, keeping my fingers away from the contaminated napkin. With my right hand, I try to drop my seventy-five cents into his open palm. But right away I see that he wants to scoop the money out of my hand.

"DON'T TOUCH MY HAND!" I holler.

"What?" he replies. Then he gets that funny look again—like he's going to explode. *I've got to escape,* I think. I turn around with my germy cone, but I can't run because there are so many kids pressing from behind.

Then it comes. Kreamy sneezes a foot away from me.

"A-A-A-A-A-A-H!" I scream as I throw my ice-cream cone in the air. It lands on a little kid's head.

"Johnny!" David yells. "What on earth are you doing? What's the matter with you?"

"GERMS!" I yell back. "I'm covered with GERMS!"

Caitlin takes me by the arm and pulls me away.

"Will you stop freaking out about germs? Running into the bathroom like a maniac every five minutes, holding everything with paper towels, splattering little kids with ice cream! You're embarrassing us!"

"If I'm embarrassing you," I snap, "then I'll go around by myself."

"Fine," says Caitlin. "And take your germs with you."

"Wait a minute, you guys," Naomi says. "My brother said to stick together. Now let's go on the Sea Serpent one more time.

"Johnny," Naomi whispers to me, "you're perfectly healthy. Don't worry so much. Try to have some fun."

"I thought we were going on the log flume," David whines.

"We can go on that later. Let's go on the Sea Serpent. There's hardly a line now." I shrug.

Waiting in line we're all kind of quiet. Caitlin doesn't say anything to me. After a while, I begin to feel a little queasy. I try to convince myself it's from the spicy fries or from standing in line under the hot sun for forty-five minutes. But maybe I actually caught something from Kreamy the sneezing clown.

By the time we've wandered through the maze of fences and made it to the boarding platform, I don't feel any better. I keep quiet, because I don't want Caitlin yelling at me again. The line keeps moving, and we keep shuffling along. Finally we climb into the roller coaster cars. I do everything I did before: secure my hat, brace my feet, and pull down the padded lap and shoulder bars using my germ-protective napkins.

"Arrrrr, matey! We meet again as I foretold."

Naomi and I turn around. That loony pirate and his six-foot parrot are right behind us. They must have jumped the line. I guess if you're a character at a theme park, you can do that.

"What's up, Kaptin?" says Naomi.

The roller coaster jerks, and we turn around.

"Here we go!" sings Naomi.

I keep my eyes shut. The roller coaster begins its rumbling climb.

HELP...

"We be goin' up! Now I can survey the entirety of me Krazy Cingdum by the C." Kaptin Phun laughs hilariously.

Sickness wells up inside of me like hot lava from a volcano. Whether it's germs that got into my lunch or just my nerves finally getting the better of me, I don't know. What I do know is that I feel awful. Suddenly it occurs to me that my mini first-aid kit might contain something for an upset stomach. It probably won't start to work right away, but I might as well give it a try. As we roll over the peak, I dig my hand into my pocket and pull out the kit. I snap it open. The roller coaster plunges downward, and the first-aid materials stream out over my shoulder. Band-Aids, gauze pads, beesting ointment—everything but medicine for an upset stomach.

"Avast, there, shipmates, whence comes this airborne trash?" the parrot squawks.

Accidentally, I let go of the tiny plastic first aid kit only to hear it smack against Kaptin Phun's face. He curses, but not like a pirate.

The rest of the ride is really rough, even worse than last time because all the junk food I ate is churning around like slop in a blender. I close my eyes. In my mind, I see the flu, the Ebola virus, and all these other germs playing in my stomach. Some of them are floating on rafts and others have sunglasses on. One of them looks like Kreamy the sneezing clown, and another like spitting Kaptin Phun. But the scariest thing is that I see my T. rexes all tied up with gags in their mouths.

"Oh, no! . . ."

I hear Naomi's voice. "Johnny, are you all right?"

The roller coaster jerks to a sudden stop. A huge wave splashes over the germs and they go under. But they stick their heads back up, laughing. They're sure having a great time in my stomach.

I open my eyes, thinking the ride is over. But it isn't. For some reason the roller coaster has stopped right over the moat. Two feet below me is filthy water filled with germs the size of lobsters.

At that moment, a voice comes over the public address system: "Attention All Passengers! The Sea Serpent Is Experiencing Minor Mechanical Problems. Please Be Patient. The Ride Will Resume in a Moment. Ship Ahoy!"

"Ahoy, schmoy!" yells Kaptin Phun. "I be a wee bit enraged at this unscheduled stoppage. Get this sea beast a-movin'!"

Kaptin Phun slashes his rubber sword in the air.

"You'll be okay," Naomi says to me. "It'll start up in a minute." I nod, thankful that the delay is giving my stomach a chance to settle. I watch a balloon go up into the sky, gradually getting tinier and tinier, until it's just a red dot. Boy, do I wish I could just grab on to that balloon and float away from this park.

Suddenly my eye catches something. A little kid is trying to crawl through a hole in the fence around the moat. He seems to be about the same age as Sammy. His parents don't see him because they're watching our roller coaster stuck on the tracks. Any minute now, the poor kid will be flopping around in that dirty muck. It doesn't matter that the roller coaster tracks don't go anywhere near that part of the moat, or that the water is only about two inches deep. The fact is, you can drown in one inch of water if you're not careful. The thought of the little kid drowning in that pool of nasty germs is just too horrible to think about. His dinosaurs are probably only lizard-sized T. rexes, newly hatched. The germs will just gobble them up.

At that moment the roller coaster starts up again, and in no time at all we're back at the boarding deck. I tear out of my seat and run like a bandit past the ride attendant.

I fight my way through the crowd, hoping to grab the little kid before he takes the plunge. But just as I arrive, he slips through the hole and plops into the two-inch-deep slime.

Before I know what I'm doing, I'm crawling in after him.

The Germs Strike Back

A normal little kid would get scared the minute he found himself standing in that mucky water. But not this kid. As soon as he hits the water, he starts laughing and splashing like he's in the world's biggest baby pool. By this time the crowd has noticed and everyone starts yelling, but the adults can't get through the small hole. The kid doesn't pay any attention to them because he's having too much fun. He doesn't realize the danger he is in. He's probably never heard of germs before.

I run after him, determined not to let him become a victim. I imagine a huge mutated germ that has been living in the moat sludge for the last ten years like a crocodile, getting fatter and fatter off the popcorn, ice cream, and soda that people have tossed in.

Suddenly I lose my footing, slip, and swallow some water. I can feel the germs bursting like fireworks as they go down my throat. If I haven't gotten a deadly disease yet, it's only a matter of time now. When I'm back on my feet, all covered with glop, I look around for the kid. Above me, it seems like five hundred people are shouting at once.

Just then, I feel someone splashing me from behind. It's him. He thinks I'm playing games. I reach down and grab his arm.

"Playtime is over!" I scold. "Now you're going to have to take a hundred baths in a row to wash off all these germs."

As I crawl back through the fence with the little kid I feel light-headed. The Sea Serpent, the fence, and the moat start spinning around me. The last thing I remember before blacking out is the little kid staring at me with a pouty expression.

A couple of minutes later, I come around. A woman in a paramedic's uniform is kneeling next to me. A crowd of people are standing around us, but the police are keeping them back.

"Thank goodness!" she says when I open my eyes. "How do you feel, young man?"

"Okay," I answer. "How's that little kid?"

"He's fine, thanks to you. You're a hero!"

Just then a reporter and a cameraman barge through the crowd. The police try to tell them to stand back, but they keep coming. Kaptin Phun is right behind them.

"We're interrupting our special report on New Jersey's greatest roller coasters to bring you this late-breaking story. Today, in the dangerous waters surrounding the terrifying Sea Serpent, this young boy saved the life of a toddler who had crawled through a hole in the fence. Kaptin Phun, as owner of the Krazy Cingdum, what do you have to say about this courageous young fellow?"

Kaptin Phun snatches the microphone. "Arrrrr, matey, this midshipman shall be receiving a lifelong pass to me Krazy Cingdum as a reward for his brave deed. And let me assure our shipmates at home that me Krazy Cingdum is as safe as it ever was. The hole in the fence was most likely made last night by some punks, but we'll be a-patchin' it up lickety-split. So come on down to me Krazy Cingdum, where the food be fun, the rides be crazy, and every little boy and girl has a chance to become a hero! Not only that, but August is Folk Music Month—"

The reporter takes the microphone away from Kaptin Phun and sticks it in my face. "What is your name, son?"

"Johnny Jarvis," I say, sitting up. The paramedic tightens the blanket around my shoulders.

"So, Johnny," says the reporter, "tell us about your adventure. The police are calling you a hero. What made you decide to plunge into the moat in the nick of time to save that helpless tot?"

To be honest, I'm not really sure why I jumped into the polluted water. "I did it without thinking. From the roller coaster I saw the little kid crawling into the moat. He looked just like my brother, Sammy, who's five and can't really swim yet. So I figured he couldn't swim either, and once I thought that, I knew I might have to jump in and get him out of there fast. And so that's what I did. I decided I was going to rescue that kid no matter what, and nothing was going to stop me, not even the germs."

"The germs?" The reporter sort of crinkles his face, like he doesn't understand.

"Sure," I say. "The germs that live in the moat, some of them almost as big as hot dogs. There were tons of them in there. But they didn't get me. I'm still alive."

The paramedics give me some antibiotics because I swallowed some dirty water. As they walk me to the park office, all the people standing around start clapping and whistling. I see Naomi and Caitlin clapping, too, and David cheering. Kaptin Phun is waving his hat and his parrot is squawking as loud as ever. I know they're clapping because I saved the little boy, but I keep pretending it's also because I've battled the germs. And won.

A Free Vacation in Pirate World

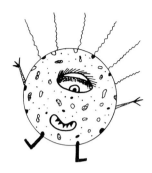

When I get home that night, Mom and Dad have already seen me on television ten times because they taped me once on the local news and kept playing it over and over. The next day we all go to Nifty Chicken for dinner to celebrate my heroic deed.

Mrs. Guildersleeve will be happy to find out that I don't think about germs as much as I did at the beginning of the summer. She'll be glad to see me doing all the things I used to do before I even knew what a germ was. I go swimming at the Dales' pool. I hike in the woods with David and Caitlin. I even play basketball with all three of them in the hot, broiling sun without worrying about heatstroke. And best of all, I hardly ever read *A Field Guide to Symptoms*.

I still think germs are scary, but if they haven't gotten me after all I've been through, I suppose I'm pretty safe for now. Besides, I'm thinking more and more about becoming a lifeguard or a rescue worker. I have to admit, worrying about people who are in trouble is a lot better than worrying about germs.

One day near the end of the summer, I get a letter of commendation in the mail, along with a lifetime pass to the Krazy Cingdum by the C. The letter is signed by Kaptin Phun, the mayor, the chief of police, and the fire chief of Seaville, New Jersey.

Kaptin Phun also gives me something else, something I never would've expected: five plane tickets and five passes to this other amusement park he owns in Florida. A brochure says Kaptin Phun's Pirate World Is Even Bigger, Krazier, and More Phun Than Krazy Cingdum in New Jersey—and we can use the passes anytime we want. Not only that, but the passes are good for a whole week. They cover our hotel rooms, too.

Of course, Mom, Dad, and Sammy jump around like we've just won the lottery. Sammy is especially happy

because he's finally going to go to an amusement park. Mom and Dad decide right then and there that we'll go during winter break, when I'm off from school.

I pretend that I'm excited, too, but when the hubbub dies down, I head upstairs and lie on my bed. It isn't that I don't want to go to Kaptin Phun's Pirate World—I really do, and I'm glad everybody is excited—but if there's one thing that can ruin a vacation, it's mechanical problems in midair. Or a pilot who falls asleep at the wheel because the darn autopilot is doing all his work for him. Or lightning zapping the wing and sending the plane into a spiral. Or making an emergency landing on a snowy mountain peak and being forced to eat seat cushions just to survive. Here I go again. . . .

Well, winter break isn't until January. That gives me almost five months to figure a way out of this new mess.

Maybe I can convince Mom and Dad that we should go to Florida by ship.